To every child who loves a special book

Copyright © 2014 by Bob Staake
All rights reserved. Published in the United States by Random House Children's Books, a division of
Random House LLC, a Penguin Random House Company, 1745 Broadway, New York, NY 10019. Random House
and the colophon are registered trademarks of Random House LLC.
Visit us on the Web! randomhouse.com/kids
Educators and librarians, for a variety of teaching tools, visit us at
RHTeachersLibrarians.com
Library of Congress Cataloging-in-Publication Data
Staake, Bob. Author, illustrator.
My pet book / by Bob Staake.
p. cm.
Summary: A boy's search for the perfect pet leads him to the bookstore, where he finds
a bright red book that becomes his best friend.
ISBN 978-0-385-37312-8 (hc) — ISBN 978-0-375-97195-2 (glb) — ISBN 978-0-375-98186-9 (ebook)
[1. Stories in rhyme. 2. Books and reading—Fiction. 3. Pets—Fiction. 4. Friendship—Fiction.] I. Title.
PZ8.3.S778My 2014
[E]—dc23
2013027525
The illustrations in this book were rendered in Adobe Photoshop.
MANUFACTURED IN CHINA
10 9 8 7 6 5 4 3 2 1
First Edition

My Pet BOOK

Bob Staake

Random House 🏠 New York

Most pets, you know, are cats and dogs.
Go out and take a look.
But there's a boy in Smartytown
Whose pet is . . . a little book.

He never cared for puppy dogs,
And kittens made him sneezy.
He pleaded with his mom and dad,
"I want a pet that's easy!"

"A book would make the perfect pet!"
He heard his mother say.
And Dad had read that no pet book
Had ever run away.

So they strolled right past the pet store
To a shop with books for sale.
Not one had whiskers, fur, or fleas,
Or a waggy little tail!

How could the boy pick out just one?
Too tough for this book lover.
But then a small book caught his eye . . .

. . . a frisky red hardcover!

Of all the books within the store,
He liked this one a lot!
The pages crisp, the printing fine,
Its spine so very taut.
He didn't need to give his pet
A name, like Rex or Spot.
It wouldn't answer anyway,
And so the book was bought!

It never ate. It never drank.
It couldn't do a trick.
It never shed. It had no fleas.
It couldn't fetch a stick.

It never needed bathing,
And its ears would never droop.
But best of all, that little pet . . .
It didn't even poop!

A better pet you couldn't have
For graceful evening strolls.
(It wasn't like those ill-bred dogs
That drink from toilet bowls,
Or like a cat that always sleeps,
Or won't turn off its purr.)
A pet book never makes a sound,
And doesn't lick its fur.

Inside the book were many tales
Of awesomeness and glory.
The boy imagined as he read
That he was *in* the story!

The boy would leave his pet book home
When off to school he'd go.

But one day when
the boy returned,

The book
was gone. . . .

"He ran away! He ran away!"
The boy began to bleat.
"How could a pet book run away
Without a pair of feet?"

The maid could hear the crying boy.
(That sound was such a rarity.)

While cleaning out the house of junk,
The maid had grabbed a box
And filled it full of household things,
Like cups and plates and socks.

The pet book must have simply been
Swept up while on the floor!
And then the maid took box and all
Straight to the old thrift store!

They raced downtown in hopes that they
Would find it on a shelf—
Just sitting there and waiting
Near a dusty Christmas elf.

It wasn't hanging with the coats,
Or sitting with the chairs!
The pet book wasn't with the lamps,
Or snoozing with stuffed bears!

Of course they went through all the books,
The new ones and the old.
The pet book wasn't anywhere.
It must have just been . . .
SOLD!

They slumped down on a musty couch,
And in unison they cried.
But then the maid leaned in and asked . . .

"Where would a pet book hide?"

The boy had never thought of that.
He broke into a smile.
He remembered something he had seen
In the dog-and-cat-stuff aisle.

"If I were just a scared pet book,
I'd likely sneak in here.
Perhaps the dark would help me hide,
And make me disappear!"

Then with his hand the boy reached in,
To feel around each nook.
And then he pulled it out to see . . .

He'd found his lost pet book!

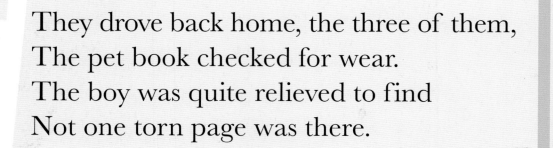

They drove back home, the three of them,
The pet book checked for wear.
The boy was quite relieved to find
Not one torn page was there.

A crazy day they'd had indeed,
Yet the story ended well.
And now the boy and his pet book
Had their very own tale to tell.

The boy's mom gently asked him
How a book could bring such joy.
"It's cuz every book's a *friend*!"
Said the yawning little boy.

His eyes were sleepy from the search
And all the time it took.
But now the boy could dream all night . . .

With his lost—and found—pet book.